RUNAWAY HAMSTER

The cage door was open and Tinkerbell was gone!

Quickly, Elizabeth looked under the beds, but there was no sign of the tiny hamster.

Elizabeth gulped. "Tinkerbell is missing."

"What?" Jessica asked.

"She must have escaped," Elizabeth explained.

Jessica got down next to Elizabeth to look in the cage. "Oh, no!" she wailed. "I didn't shut the door tightly enough! You told me to click the door shut but when Steven called me I guess I just forgot to close the cage. What are we going to do?"

SWEET VALLEY KIDS

RUNAWAY HAMSTER

Written by
Molly Mia Stewart

Created by
FRANCINE PASCAL

Illustrated by
Ying-Hwa Hu

A BANTAM SKYLARK BOOK®
NEW YORK · TORONTO · LONDON · SYDNEY · AUCKLAND

RL 2, 005-008

RUNAWAY HAMSTER
A Bantam Skylark Book / November 1989

Sweet Valley High® and Sweet Valley Kids
are trademarks of Francine Pascal.

Conceived by Francine Pascal
Produced by Daniel Weiss Associates, Inc.,
27 West 20th Street,
New York, NY 10011

Cover art by Susan Tang.

Skylark Books is a registered trademark of Bantam Books, a division of
Bantam Doubleday Dell Publishing Group, Inc.

ISBN 0-553-15759-0

Published simultaneously in the United States and Canada

Bantam Books are published by Bantam Books, a division of Bantam Doubleday Dell Publishing Group, Inc. Its trademark, consisting of the words
"Bantam Books" and the portrayal of a rooster, is Registered in U.S. Patent
and Trademark Office and in other countries. Marca Registrada. Bantam
Books, 666 Fifth Avenue, New York, New York 10103.

PRINTED IN THE UNITED STATES OF AMERICA

0 9 8 7 6 5 4 3 2 1

To Mia Pascal Johansson

CHAPTER 1

The Class Hamster

Jessica Wakefield was standing in Mrs. Becker's second grade class before class began. She was staring at Tinkerbell, the class hamster. She was glad that Tinkerbell was safely inside a cage.

Tinkerbell looked out at Jessica. She picked up a sunflower seed in her tiny paws and nibbled on it. Then she jumped onto her wheel. *Squeak-squeak-squeak-squeak.*

It was a horrible sound. Jessica made a face. She didn't like Tinkerbell *at all*.

"I wonder who Mrs. Becker will pick this

time," Lila Fowler said. Lila was looking at Tinkerbell from the other side of the cage.

Each week a different student was chosen to take Tinkerbell home for the weekend. That way Tinkerbell never got lonely. Today was the day before the holiday break, and whoever was chosen would get to keep Tinkerbell for a long time.

Jessica hadn't been picked yet, and she hoped she never would be. "I don't want her in my house," she said to Lila. "She's just an ugly rat."

"No she's not," Lila replied. "Anyway, you'd keep her in the cage!"

Jessica shivered. "She could always get out and bite me." She shook her head again. "Maybe I can tell Mrs. Becker I have allergies."

"Tinkerbell's allergic to you," Charlie Cashman said.

"Very funny," Jessica grumbled. Lila put her nose in the air and pretended Charlie wasn't even there.

"OK, class! Take your seats!" Mrs. Becker called. "It's time to see who's going to get Tinkerbell for vacation!"

Some boys made pretend gagging sounds when she said "Tinkerbell." They all thought Tinkerbell was a silly name.

Mrs. Becker took a shoe box out of her desk drawer. Inside were slips of paper. Each slip had a name on it.

Caroline Pearce raised her hand. "Can somebody pick it for you?" she called. She was always asking to erase the blackboard or pass out art supplies.

"Thanks, but I think I'll do it," Mrs. Becker answered.

Please don't pick me, Jessica wished silently. She crossed her fingers and closed her eyes tightly.

"Don't let it be my turn," she whispered out loud.

"What did you say?" her twin sister, Elizabeth, asked.

Jessica opened one eye and looked at Elizabeth, who was sitting next to her. They always sat together in class.

Jessica and Elizabeth Wakefield were sisters. And they were twins. They looked exactly alike. Both girls had long blond hair with bangs and blue-green eyes. They were the only identical twins at Sweet Valley Elementary School. Plus, they were best friends.

Jessica thought being twins was fun, especially when they tried to fool people. Sometimes they wore the same outfits to school and then no one could tell them apart during the day. Only the name bracelets they wore on their wrists let people know who was who.

Even though they were twins, Jessica and Elizabeth were different in many ways. Jessica liked to whisper and pass notes in class. She didn't like to do homework and always tried to get out of doing her chores. Elizabeth was very responsible and loved school. She paid attention in class. She enjoyed reading mystery books and writing short poems.

Elizabeth was eager to get Tinkerbell and to take care of her for vacation. Jessica was afraid of animals and didn't especially like the responsibility of having a pet.

"I hope it's not one of us," Jessica said.

Elizabeth opened her eyes wide. "I want to get picked! I want a turn with Tinkerbell!"

"No!" Jessica squeezed her eyes shut again. Then she peeked at her sister. Elizabeth was crossing her fingers, too, but she was hoping for just the opposite of what Jessica wished for. So Jessica crossed her arms and then her feet for extra luck.

"Me, me, me," Elizabeth whispered.

"No, no, no," Jessica whispered.

"Is everybody ready?" Mrs. Becker asked.

"Ready!" the class shouted.

Mrs. Becker opened the shoe box and closed her eyes. Then she reached inside.

Jessica held her breath. Elizabeth held her breath.

Mrs. Becker pulled out a piece of paper. She unfolded it very slowly.

"Elizabeth Wakefield!" she read.

Jessica screamed. "No!"

Elizabeth clapped her hands. "Hooray! We get to take Tinkerbell!"

"Since it's going to be winter vacation," Mrs. Becker went on, "I think Jessica should share the responsibility with you, Elizabeth."

Jessica made a face. "Yuck," she said softly so the teacher wouldn't hear.

"Tinkerbell will starve if Jessica has to feed her," Winston Egbert shouted.

Jessica looked over at her twin sister. Elizabeth was smiling at her. Jessica loved sharing almost everything with her twin, but this was one thing she did not want any part of!

CHAPTER 2

Part of the Family

Elizabeth carried Tinkerbell's cage onto the school bus. All the kids crowded around.

"Look, everyone!" Crystal Burton said. "Isn't it *cute*?"

"Where'd you get the hamster?" Melanie Mills asked. Melanie and Crystal were both third graders.

"She's our class pet," Elizabeth explained. "We're taking care of her over the vacation."

"Not me," Jessica corrected. "Just Liz."

Tinkerbell began to thump her foot up and down.

As everyone crowded around, Elizabeth pulled the cage closer to her. She wanted to protect Tinkerbell. "She's a little scared, so don't get too close."

Their older brother, Steven, got onto the bus. Usually he pretended not to see them, but this time he stopped.

"Hey, what's that?" he asked, pointing at the cage.

"Tinkerbell," Elizabeth said. "We get her for the whole vacation." She put the cage down on the seat next to her.

Jessica slumped down and crossed her arms. She sat as far away from the cage as she could without falling off the seat.

When they got home, Elizabeth took Tinkerbell upstairs to their bedroom. Jessica followed.

"Where should we put the cage?" Elizabeth asked.

Jessica wrinkled her forehead. "Maybe she should stay in the basement. She'd be happier down there."

"No!" Elizabeth looked upset. "I want her in our room so I can make sure she's OK."

Jessica picked up her stuffed koala and hugged it. "Suppose she gets out," she said. "She might come into my bed while I'm sleeping and bite me."

"She won't," Elizabeth said. She put the cage down between their beds. "We'll keep her inside the cage all the time." Tinkerbell crouched in one corner of the cage and twitched her whiskers.

Jessica leaned over the side of her bed and looked inside the cage. "I think she's telling us she doesn't like it there, Liz."

"Yes, she does," Elizabeth replied. She knelt down in front of the cage. "Don't you, Tinkerbell?"

The hamster hopped onto the wheel and started running. *Squeak-squeak-squeak-squeak.*

"That wheel sure is noisy," Jessica said after a moment. "It's going to keep me awake all night."

Elizabeth frowned. The wheel was loud.

"Maybe she'll sleep at night when we do," she said.

Jessica moved her bed a few inches closer to the wall. She sat on the edge and wouldn't look at Tinkerbell.

Elizabeth pretended not to notice. Sometimes Jessica was very stubborn.

"I'm going to feed her and give her lots of water," Elizabeth said. "I'm going to take really good care of her."

Jessica just sat there, pouting.

They heard footsteps in the hallway.

"Hi, girls." Mrs. Wakefield came into the room. "No snack today? You came right up to your room."

"We got stuck with this disgusting thing for the whole vacation," Jessica complained. "Isn't that terrible?"

Mrs. Wakefield looked into the cage and smiled.

"Oh, yes. Mrs. Becker wrote to all the parents about Tinkerbell. We told her it would be perfectly fine for you two to take care of her."

"Thanks, Mom," Elizabeth said. "She's going to love it here. She'll be just like one of the family. We're going to take good care of her."

"Not me," Jessica said grumpily.

Mrs. Wakefield looked surprised. "No, Jessica. You have to do your share of the work, too."

Jessica didn't look up. She started arranging her dolls and stuffed animals on her bed.

Elizabeth looked at her sister. Having a pet was a big responsibility. But it was also going to be lots of fun. Jessica often wouldn't do her share of the chores unless their mother reminded her. Maybe Jessica really wouldn't help with Tinkerbell. And if she did, Elizabeth hoped Jessica wouldn't treat Tinkerbell badly.

Just in case, Elizabeth decided to check on the hamster when it was Jessica's turn. That way, if Jessica forgot anything, Tinkerbell would be OK.

CHAPTER 3

A New Friend

Every day, Elizabeth gave Tinkerbell fresh water and new seeds. She liked playing with the hamster, too. Tinkerbell had soft fur and pretty brown eyes. Elizabeth even let Tinkerbell crawl up her arm. It tickled.

Jessica still wouldn't go near the hamster. Whenever Elizabeth opened the cage, Jessica would run out of the room.

One day, Elizabeth invited Amy Sutton over. Amy was her second-best friend, after Jessica.

"Let's play with Tinkerbell and let her run

around in the bathtub," Amy suggested. "I did that when I had my turn with her."

Elizabeth smiled. "What a great idea. She can't climb out, because the tub is too high and slippery."

They went upstairs and Elizabeth carefully opened the door of Tinkerbell's cage. She didn't want to frighten the hamster. "Come on, Tink," she said. "Want to go on a trip?"

Amy giggled. Together, they brought Tinkerbell into the bathroom. When Elizabeth placed her gently in the tub, Tinkerbell began to scamper around. She sniffed at the drain.

"I think she likes it," Amy said.

Elizabeth agreed. "She's having fun. I wish I could have a hamster all the time."

"Me, too," Amy said. "I wish I could have a dog and a cat and a horse *and* a hamster."

Elizabeth laughed. She let Tinkerbell run across her hand.

"She's just the right size for your dollhouse," Amy said. "Wouldn't it be fun if she could live in it?"

"I don't think Jessica would like that," Elizabeth said. "But we could bring some of the furniture in here. I'll be right back!"

While Amy guarded Tinkerbell, Elizabeth ran back into the bedroom. The twins had a big dollhouse filled with furniture. Elizabeth took out a miniature canopy bed, a sofa with real cushions, and the removable sink. She carried them back into the bathroom.

Elizabeth and Amy set up the furniture in the bathtub and Tinkerbell climbed onto the bed. It was just the right size. Then Tinkerbell started nibbling on one of the bedposts.

"Uh-oh!" Elizabeth poked Tinkerbell gently with her finger. "Don't do that, Tink!"

Tinkerbell looked like the animals Elizabeth used to read about in her storybooks. Mice and rabbits in books always lived in miniature houses with tiny furniture. Elizabeth thought it would be fun to write her own story about Tinkerbell living in the dollhouse.

The girls heard voices in the bedroom. It was Jessica and Lila.

"Come in here!" Elizabeth called out. "Look at what we're doing!"

Jessica and Lila came into the bathroom. When Jessica saw the dollhouse furniture in the tub, she screamed. "She's eating the bed! Now I'll never be able to play with that stuff again."

Amy crossed her eyes at Jessica. "Tinkerbell is really cute! She didn't ruin anything."

"Yes she did," Jessica said. She folded her arms. "And she's so messy. I can see little seeds all over the bedroom!"

Lila shrugged. "I know. But I still can't wait for my turn."

"You can have my turn right now," Jessica said.

Elizabeth was positive that if Jessica gave Tinkerbell a chance, she'd like the hamster. But Jessica didn't even want to try.

CHAPTER 4

Feeding Time

On Saturday Jessica and Elizabeth watched TV after breakfast.

"Jessica, isn't it your turn to feed Tinkerbell today?" Mrs. Wakefield asked.

Jessica wished her mother would forget which day it was. She didn't want to go near the hamster. She stared at the TV screen.

"Jessica?" Mrs. Wakefield said.

"Yes, it's my turn," Jessica mumbled.

Elizabeth stood up. "I'll do it if Jess doesn't want to, Mom."

Mrs. Wakefield shook her head. "No, I'd like Jessica to do her share."

"OK," Jessica said. She dragged herself up the stairs.

"Are you hungry now?" Jessica grumbled as she entered her room.

She got down on the floor and looked into Tinkerbell's cage. She wished she didn't have to open the door and put her hand inside. Tinkerbell might touch her.

Tinkerbell's bed was a toilet-paper tube with pieces of tissue inside. Jessica had to agree it looked very cozy.

The hamster poked her head out of the tube. Her whiskers wiggled. Then she crawled out.

Jessica made a face.

"You do look like a rat," she whispered. Since no one else was in the room, Jessica stuck her tongue out at the hamster.

Tinkerbell went to the water bottle and took a drink. Bubbles went up through the liquid. The bottle was almost empty.

"I guess I have to get you some more water," Jessica said. "Plus some food."

She opened the bag of food Mrs. Becker had given them. Inside were tiny round yellow seeds, long gray seeds, black-and-white striped seeds, hard kernels of corn and some peanuts.

"Yuck," Jessica said.

Carefully, she opened the cage door and reached inside. Tinkerbell ran to the opposite corner. Her whiskers wiggled around some more.

Jessica quickly grabbed the seed dish and poured some food into it.

At that moment, Steven called from down the hall.

"Jess!" he shouted. "Come here!"

Jessica placed the dish back inside the cage. "Why?"

"Just come here!" he shouted again.

Jessica pushed the door shut and ran down the hall to Steven's room.

"What do you want?"

Steven was sitting at his desk. In front of him was an empty shoe box. A stick held up one end and Jessica could see a piece of cheese underneath.

"Let me try this out," he said.

Jessica frowned. "What is it?"

"It's a mousetrap I made for science class," her brother said. He grinned his mischievous kind of smile. "I want to see if it works on your hamster."

Jessica opened her eyes wide. "No!"

26

"It won't hurt," he said. "It just traps them."

"No, no, no," Jessica repeated. "Not in a million, billion, zillion years."

Even though Jessica didn't like Tinkerbell, she didn't want to put her in a mousetrap. Besides, if they took Tinkerbell out of her cage, she might get away.

"I *promise* it won't hurt her," Steven said again. He crossed his heart and snapped his fingers twice.

Jessica wasn't sure she should believe him. But he had made their special promise sign. "*Promise?*"

He nodded slowly. "I promise."

CHAPTER 5

Runaway Hamster

Elizabeth wasn't paying attention to the TV show. She kept wondering if Jessica would follow the instructions she had given her on how to feed Tinkerbell. After waiting for a few minutes, she decided to go up and check.

She ran upstairs. Jessica wasn't in their bedroom. "Hi, Tinkerbell," Elizabeth called out as she entered the room.

She got down on her knees and looked in the cage. What she saw—or rather, what she didn't see—made her gasp.

The cage door was open and Tinkerbell was gone!

Quickly, Elizabeth looked under the beds, but there was no sign of the tiny hamster.

Just then Jessica walked back in. "You know what Steven wants to do?" she said.

Elizabeth just stared at her sister. She was too shocked to say anything.

"He wants to put Tinkerbell in a trap," Jessica went on. She flopped onto her bed. "I told him no."

Then she saw Elizabeth's expression. "What's wrong?"

Elizabeth gulped. "Tinkerbell is missing."

"What?" Jessica looked confused.

"She must have escaped," Elizabeth explained.

Jessica got down next to Elizabeth to look in the cage. "Oh, no!" she wailed. "I didn't shut the door tightly enough! You told me to click the door shut but when Steven called me I guess I just forgot. What are we going to do?"

"We have to find her," Elizabeth said. She bit her fingernail. "She doesn't really belong to us."

Jessica jumped back onto her bed and curled her legs up. "Don't let her get me! She might get under the covers!"

"Stop it!" Elizabeth said. She wished Jessica didn't hate Tinkerbell so much.

Jessica looked upset. "I don't want to get in trouble," she said in a frightened voice. "Mom is going to be so angry at me!"

"Not if we find Tinkerbell first." Elizabeth looked at the cage. "If we find her, we won't even have to tell Mom Tinkerbell got away."

Jessica sniffled. She looked like she might start to cry. "Really?"

Elizabeth stood up and took Jessica's hand. "Let's try to find her right now."

"OK," Jessica said. "Where should we look first?" She carefully picked up some of her stuffed animals and looked under them.

"I already checked under the beds," Elizabeth explained. "Let's look everywhere else."

The twins searched the whole room. Elizabeth looked in the closet, even inside all of the shoes. Jessica opened a desk drawer. She saw the barrettes she had lost last week, but no hamster.

Next they went down the hall to their parents' bedroom. Jessica hoped Tinkerbell was in there. They searched every inch, but no Tinkerbell.

The girls walked back to their room. "What if we don't find her, Lizzie?" Jessica said.

Elizabeth looked at her sister and took a deep breath. "We just have to keep looking till we do."

CHAPTER 6

Jessica's Plan

They searched for one hour but there was still no sign of Tinkerbell. The twins gave up. Tinkerbell had disappeared.

Jessica and Elizabeth went outside to their favorite pine tree. They always went there when they wanted to be alone.

"She must be in the house *somewhere*," Jessica said. "I hope she doesn't get into our closet."

Elizabeth sat down on the ground. She picked up a pine needle. "I just hope she didn't get outside."

Jessica made sure there weren't any worms or bugs on the ground. Then she sat next to Elizabeth. She felt terrible. When everyone found out she lost Tinkerbell, she was going to be in big trouble.

"I didn't mean for her to escape," she said.

"Poor Tinkerbell," Elizabeth said sadly. "I wonder if she's scared."

"Liz!" Jessica gasped and grabbed Elizabeth's hand.

"What?" Elizabeth said.

Jessica leaned close to Elizabeth and whispered, "I just thought of something. A really, really good idea!"

Elizabeth rolled her eyes toward the sky. Jessica was always full of ideas that never worked. "What?"

"Don't all hamsters look alike?"

Elizabeth's eyes widened. "Uh-huh. So?"

"We could get another one," Jessica went on. "Another hamster would look just like Tinkerbell."

"But, Jessica," Elizabeth said. "That won't work."

"Why not? No one will be able to tell the difference." Jessica said.

Elizabeth wasn't sure it was a good plan. She chewed on a piece of her blond hair and frowned. "It's like telling a lie, Jess," she said.

"But, Liz!" Jessica's voice was shaky. "Everyone will be so angry at me! Everyone will hate me!" She blinked hard as if she were going to cry.

Elizabeth looked upset. She grabbed Jessica's hand. "Don't cry, Jess!"

Jessica blinked some more until real tears came. "I promise it will work," she said sniffling.

"Do you really think so?" Elizabeth asked.

Jessica nodded. She crossed her heart and snapped her fingers two times. Then she sat closer to her twin. "No one can tell *us* apart."

"I guess they wouldn't be able to tell two hamsters apart," Elizabeth said slowly.

Jessica squeezed Elizabeth's hand. "Isn't it a good idea?"

"I guess so," Elizabeth agreed.

"Good." Jessica felt a lot better. All their problems were solved.

Now she wouldn't get into trouble. It was a perfect plan.

CHAPTER 7

Mom to the Rescue

Elizabeth and Jessica ran inside, up the stairs, and into their bedroom. Jessica closed the door. "How much money do we have?" she asked.

Elizabeth emptied her bunny bank onto her bed and spread out a quarter, two dimes, plus six pennies. She counted the coins under her breath. "Fifty-one cents."

Jessica took a pink satin change purse out of her night table drawer and turned it upside down. A string bracelet, a piece of glass that looked like a real diamond, and a nickel fell out.

"How much does a hamster cost?" Elizabeth whispered.

"I don't know," Jessica whispered back. "I don't think we have enough."

"What are we going to do?"

Jessica looked disappointed. She scrunched up her satin purse. Then she slowly shook her head from side to side. "I don't know," she said gloomily.

Elizabeth looked at the empty cage on the floor. She had promised to look after Tinkerbell, and now the poor little creature was gone. She felt like crying. "We'd better tell Mom."

"No!" Jessica said quickly. "We can't!"

"But we have to!" Elizabeth looked at her

twin sister. "You didn't do it on purpose. You made a mistake. You won't get punished for it. Besides, we can't get a new hamster if we don't have enough money."

After a few seconds, Jessica nodded very slowly. "You're right. Mom will know what to do."

Elizabeth knew Jessica was afraid of getting in trouble. "Come on. We'll tell her together."

Mrs. Wakefield was downstairs reading a book in the family room. Elizabeth and Jessica stopped in the doorway. Neither one of them said anything.

Their mother looked up. "Hi, girls. What's up?"

The twins looked at each other. Then Elizabeth nudged Jessica with her elbow.

"Mom?" Jessica began in a squeaky voice.

"Yes, dear?"

"Um . . ." Jessica's face was pink. "Um . . ."

Elizabeth felt sorry for her sister, so she spoke up. "Mom, we lost Tinkerbell," she said. "We can't find her *anywhere*."

Mrs. Wakefield put her book down. "You—what?"

"And we want to buy a new one to take to school after vacation," Elizabeth added. "So can you please help us?"

Jessica burst into tears. "I didn't mean it!" she sobbed. "I just forgot to shut the door tightly!"

Elizabeth looked at her sister. Sometimes Jessica pretended to cry to get attention. This time she looked like she really *was* crying.

"Oh, dear," Mrs. Wakefield said. "I'm sure

you feel terrible about what happened, Jessica. We'll buy a new hamster. But I want you both to promise you'll explain to Mrs. Becker what happened."

"We will," Elizabeth said. "We're really sorry."

"I know you're sorry," their mother said. "Don't cry, girls. I'm not angry at you." She held out both hands.

Jessica stopped crying. She smiled.

"Mom, you're the best," Elizabeth cried.

"Now, come on," Mrs. Wakefield said. "We'll go to the pet store right now."

Mrs. Wakefield hugged them both. "Go get Tinkerbell's cage. We can bring the new hamster home in it."

The twins hugged each other and ran upstairs. The problem didn't seem so bad anymore now that Mrs. Wakefield was helping them solve it.

But Elizabeth still felt worried about Tinkerbell. Where was she?

CHAPTER 8

The New Tinkerbell

Jessica felt nervous on Monday morning. It was the first day of school after vacation. The new hamster looked just like Tinkerbell, but soon everyone would know the truth.

She was carrying the cage because her mother told her she had to. She was trying to keep it as far away from her as she could. She didn't like the new hamster any more than she had liked Tinkerbell.

"Do we really have to tell Mrs. Becker?"

she asked Elizabeth when they had settled in their seats on the school bus.

Elizabeth stuck a finger through the cage wires. The new hamster sniffed it. Elizabeth looked serious. "Yes."

Jessica moved closer to her twin. "But everyone will know what I did," she said. "And they'll be mad at me."

"We have to tell the truth," her sister replied. "We promised."

"OK." Jessica felt grumpy and worried at the same time. She slumped down in her seat.

When they got to school, Jessica was the last one off the bus.

"Why are you walking so slowly?" Elizabeth asked.

"This cage is heavy," Jessica explained.

Jessica really didn't want to tell Mrs.

Becker what had happened. She wished it would take forever to get there.

Elizabeth waited by the door of their classroom. Jessica walked by her with the cage.

"Tinkerbell!" Lois Waller ran over to Jessica.

Jessica backed up.

"Hi, Tinkerbell!" Lois said to the new hamster. "You are so lucky, Jessica. I haven't had my turn yet."

"Was it fun to have her?" Sandra Ferris asked. "I love Tinkerbell."

Jessica wanted to run away. Pretty soon, everyone would hate her. It was all Tinkerbell's fault, too. She wished she had never seen a hamster in her whole life.

Mrs. Becker was putting books on a shelf. She turned around. "Well! Our hamster is home safe and sound from vacation. Thank you for taking such good care of her, girls," she said.

The new hamster twitched her nose. She looked up at everyone through the bars of the cage.

"Why doesn't she jump on the wheel?" Todd Wilkins asked. He was bending over to look at the hamster.

"Yeah, Tinkerbell always goes on that dumb wheel," Winston Egbert added. He held his hands over his ears. "Squeak, squeak, squeak."

Jessica's chin trembled. "Maybe she's tired," she whispered.

Ellen Riteman said in a baby voice, "Are you sweepy, Tinkybell?"

Jessica looked at Elizabeth again. Her twin's face was bright pink.

"Did you have any trouble with Tinker-bell?" Mrs. Becker asked.

Jessica looked up. No one would ever like her again. A tear rolled down her face.

"What's wrong?" Mrs. Becker asked quickly.

Jessica held out the cage. "This isn't Tinkerbell!"

CHAPTER 9

The Terrible Truth

Elizabeth's stomach did a flip-flop. She felt awful for Jessica as her sister tried to explain.

"But where is the real Tinkerbell?" Sandra Ferris asked.

Lois began to cry. She cried at almost everything.

"Oh, no," Ellen said. Other kids gathered around to see what was happening. "Is she OK?"

"Where did who go?" Lila asked .

Ellen pointed to the cage. "That's not Tinkerbell! Jessica *lost* her!"

Jessica began to cry. Mrs. Becker took the cage out of Jessica's hands and put it on a table.

Elizabeth held Jessica's hand. She thought she was going to cry, too.

"This hamster isn't half as good as Tinkerbell," Winston said in a loud voice. "It just sits there."

The whole class crowded around the new hamster. The hamster looked frightened, and ran inside the toilet-paper tube. Elizabeth felt awful.

"Tinkerbell was much better," Lila agreed.

"Now, girls, can you explain what happened?" Mrs. Becker asked. She didn't look angry. Her eyes did look red, though, and she sniffled as if she had a cold.

Jessica tried to stop crying, but big tears ran down her cheeks.

"Tinkerbell escaped, and we couldn't find her," Elizabeth explained. "We thought we should get a new hamster because it was our fault."

Mrs. Becker put her arm around Elizabeth's shoulder. "That was very thoughtful of you. I think this is a nice hamster, too."

"I'll bet it wasn't *your* fault," Todd said to Elizabeth. "I know *you* took good care of Tinkerbell."

Everyone in class knew Elizabeth was very responsible. But Elizabeth didn't want to blame Jessica. "But, Mrs. Becker?" she went on. "What about the real Tinkerbell? Will she be OK?"

Todd opened his eyes wide. "Yeah, what if a cat gets her?"

Ellen screamed at the thought. Lila opened her mouth, but didn't say anything.

"You know what?" Charlie said in a loud voice. "My cat Spike looked fatter this morning. He didn't eat any of his cat food, either."

"He ate Tinkerbell?" Caroline said. "Mrs. Becker! Charlie's cat ate Tinkerbell!"

"Please calm down, everyone," Mrs. Becker said.

Tom McKay spoke up. "Maybe she's still hiding in your house."

That made Elizabeth feel better, but Jessica squeezed her eyes shut and said, "Eewww!"

"Now, now!" Mrs. Becker held up her hands for quiet. "Our part of California is a perfect environment for hamsters," she said.

Elizabeth gulped. "Really?"

"Yes. If Tinkerbell got outside, she'll just

be a wild hamster, that's all," the teacher explained.

"You mean, like a mouse?" Amy asked. Her nose was red.

Mrs. Becker nodded. "That's right. She'll be just fine. She'll find a nice hole somewhere safe."

Elizabeth felt a little bit better, but she kept worrying about Tinkerbell.

Maybe Tinkerbell is still in the house somewhere, she thought. *We've got to find her.*

Otherwise, Elizabeth would wonder where Tinkerbell was forever.

CHAPTER 10

A Mouse in the House

Jessica and Elizabeth were having their after-school snacks in the kitchen. Jessica blew bubbles through a straw in her milk. It wasn't as much fun as usual, though.

"I think Thumbelina is a nice name," Elizabeth said.

"I guess," Jessica said.

The class had agreed to name the new hamster Thumbelina. But Jessica didn't like the name. Thumbelina just reminded her of Tinkerbell. Jessica took a small sip of milk.

The twins heard a car door slam shut in the driveway.

"It's Dad!" Elizabeth said.

Mr. Wakefield had been away on business. The twins had missed him very much.

"He's home!" Jessica yelled. She ran to the back door just as it opened.

"Dad!" Jessica and Elizabeth screamed at the same time.

Mr. Wakefield laughed. He gave them both a big hug. "How are the two prettiest girls in Sweet Valley?"

"Fine, Daddy," Elizabeth said happily.

Jessica looked at her sister. She didn't want her father to know about Tinkerbell. She wanted to forget all about the hamsters.

"What are you pumpkins eating?" their father asked. He rubbed his hands together. "Cookies and milk?"

Jessica nodded. "Yup. Want some?"

"I think I'll have crackers instead," he said.

Mrs. Wakefield came into the kitchen and kissed Mr. Wakefield hello.

"How was your trip?" she asked.

"Good. But I'm starved," he answered.

Mr. Wakefield opened a door under the counter. He took out a box of crackers and turned it upside down. He frowned.

"What's wrong, Dad?" Jessica asked.

Mr. Wakefield looked surprised. "It looks as if we have mice," he announced.

Jessica's stomach jumped. Her eyes opened wide. "What do you mean, Dad?"

He showed them the box. "Something chewed a hole in the bottom."

Jessica looked at Elizabeth. Elizabeth looked at Jessica. Then Jessica looked at her

mother. Mrs. Wakefield smiled. "Tinkerbell?" Jessica whispered.

"Who's Tinkerbell?" their father asked.

"We'll explain later," Mrs. Wakefield said.

Elizabeth was smiling from ear to ear. "She's still here!"

Jessica jumped out of her chair. "Come on! We have to find her!"

CHAPTER 11

Twin Hamsters

Elizabeth opened all the cabinets in the kitchen. She looked behind everything on the shelves. Jessica looked in the silverware drawer.

"Do you think it's really Tinkerbell?" Elizabeth wondered. She was beginning to feel excited.

"Of course it is," her sister said. "Unless you think it's Steven." Both girls giggled.

Jessica looked in the garbage pail.

"Did you check the refrigerator?" their father asked.

"Dad!" Elizabeth gave him a stern look. "She can't get in there. How could she open the door?"

Mr. Wakefield held up his hands. "I still don't know who we're talking about!"

"Our class hamster," Jessica explained. "She got loose in the house."

Mr. Wakefield laughed. "I see."

"It's not funny, Daddy," Elizabeth scolded. "She's so little!"

Elizabeth opened the drawer where her mother kept herbs and spices. But Tinkerbell wasn't there.

"She might not be in the kitchen anymore," Mrs. Wakefield pointed out. "She could be anywhere."

"But where?" Elizabeth bit her lip.

"Come quickly, everyone!" Steven yelled from upstairs. "I caught something!"

66

Elizabeth stared at Jessica. Then they both ran to the staircase.

"I caught something in my mousetrap!" Steven shouted.

Elizabeth's heart pounded. She couldn't wait to see what it was.

The shoe box on Steven's desk wasn't propped up anymore. It was lying flat and now it started to move.

"See?" Steven said. His brown eyes looked excited. "Something's in there!"

Elizabeth and Jessica ran to the desk. Carefully, Elizabeth lifted up the box.

They saw two dark eyes and long whiskers. "Tinkerbell!" Elizabeth shouted.

The hamster crawled out from under the box. She stood up on her hind legs and sniffed.

Then Tinkerbell started to scamper toward the edge of the desk.

"Get her!" Steven yelled. "She'll fall off!"

Jessica jumped forward. She put both hands around the little hamster and picked her up.

"Here," Elizabeth said, holding out her hands. "I'll take her." She knew Jessica wouldn't want to hold the hamster for very long.

But Jessica kept Tinkerbell. She was starting to smile. "Hey!" she giggled. "Her whiskers are tickly." She laughed. "She's soft, too."

Elizabeth was surprised. "Do you like her now?"

"I think so," Jessica said. She peeked at Tinkerbell through her fingers. "She's pretty nice. I didn't know she was so soft."

"I knew you would like her," Elizabeth said.

Jessica petted Tinkerbell with one finger. "I guess she won't bite me," she said.

"My trap works!" Steven said proudly. "I told you it wouldn't hurt her. I can't wait to tell my teacher."

"Neither can we," Elizabeth giggled.

The next day, Elizabeth and Jessica took Tinkerbell to school. She was in the same shoe box that had been her trap.

"Mrs. Becker?" Jessica stood in front of the teacher's desk. Elizabeth stood next to her.

"Yes?" Mrs. Becker said, looking at the box. "Did you bring something to show the class?" Mrs. Becker looked very sleepy. She took a tissue out of her purse to blow her nose.

Caroline, Lila, and Sandra crowded around. Some of the boys were looking at

Jim Sturbridge's sticker collection, but they came over, too.

"What is it?" Lila asked.

"What's in the box?" Todd wanted to know.

Jessica giggled. "Show them," she whispered to her sister. "It's Tinkerbell. We found her!"

Elizabeth lifted up the lid. Tinkerbell put her paws on the edge of the box.

"Look! It's the real Tinkerbell!" Sandra cried.

Mrs. Becker carried Tinkerbell to the cage and put her inside with Thumbelina.

"Now Tinkerbell won't be lonely anymore," Mrs. Becker said. "She has a friend."

Ricky Capaldo looked into the cage. "I can't wait for my turn," he said. "Now we get to take two hamsters home!"

"That's right," Amy said. "I hope I can get another turn soon."

Andy Franklin squinted at the hamsters, and then at Elizabeth. "They look just the same."

Lila giggled. "They're identical twins."

Elizabeth smiled at Jessica. "Just like us."

"Two of a kind," Mrs. Becker added. Then she sneezed.

"Bless you," Andy said politely.

Mrs. Becker smiled. "Thank you, Andy."

"Do you have a cold, Mrs. Becker?" Jessica asked.

"Yeah!" Winston said, his eyes sparkling. "If you have to stay home, Mrs. Becker, then we'll get a substitute teacher." He looked at Charlie Cashman and smiled. They both remembered the fun they had had the last time Mrs. Becker had been ill.

"Now, now, I'm just fine," Mrs. Becker declared. "*Achoo!*" She took out another tissue and blew her nose.

Elizabeth shook her head. She didn't think Mrs. Becker looked fine. In fact, Elizabeth thought Mrs. Becker looked terrible.

*What will the twins and their classmates discover after Mrs. Becker is out sick? Find out in Sweet Valley Kids #3, **THE SUBSTITUTE TEACHER**.*

ENTER SWEET VALLEY KIDS™ DREAM BIRTHDAY GIFT SWEEPSTAKES

OFFICIAL RULES:

1. *No Purchase is Necessary.* Enter by completing the Official Entry Form (or handprinting your name, age, address, telephone number and dream birthday gift on a plain 3" x 5" card) and sending it to:

SWEET VALLEY KIDS™ SWEEPSTAKES
BANTAM BOOKS
% YR Marketing
666 Fifth Avenue
New York, New York 10103

2.   1 Grand Prize: A dream birthday gift, including a bicycle, dollhouse, or ballet outfit, or another gift of your choice (maximum retail value: $500.00).

  25 First Prizes: Libraries of popular Bantam titles (approximate retail value: $35.00).

  20 Second Prizes: Makeup kits to include an assortment of makeup items (approximate retail value: $20.00).

3.   Sweepstakes begins October 1, 1989 and all entries must be postmarked and received by Bantam no later than January 15, 1990. Winners will be chosen by Bantam's Young Readers Marketing Department by a random drawing from all completed entries on or about February 15, 1990 and will be notified by mail on or about March 15, 1990. Bantam's decision is final. Winners have 30 days from date of notice in which to accept their prize award or an alternate winner will be chosen. A prize won by a minor will be awarded to a parent or legal guardian. Odds of winning depend on the number of completed entries received. All prizes will be awarded. Enter as often as you wish, but each entry must be mailed separately, and none will be returned. No prize substitution, mechanically reproduced entries, or transfers allowed. Limit one prize per household or address. Bantam is not responsible for incomplete or lost or misdirected entries.

4.   Prize winners and their parents or legal guardians may be required to execute an Affidavit of Eligibility and Promotional Release supplied by Bantam. Entering the sweepstakes constitutes permission for use of winner's name, address and likeness for publicity and promotional purposes, with no additional compensation.

5.   Employees of Bantam Books, Bantam Doubleday Dell Publishing Group, Inc., their subsidiaries and affiliates, and their immediate family members are not eligible to enter this sweepstakes. This sweepstakes is open to residents of the U.S. and Canada, excluding the Province of Quebec. A Canadian winner may be required to correctly answer an arithmetical skill-testing question in order to receive the prize. Void where prohibited or restricted by law. All federal, state and local regulations apply. Taxes, if any, are the winner's sole responsibility.

6.   For a list of the winners, send a stamped, self-addressed envelope entirely separate from your entry to "THE SWEET VALLEY KIDS™ SWEEPSTAKES" WINNERS LIST, Bantam Books, Dept. JJ-L, 666 Fifth Avenue, 23rd Floor, New York, New York 10103.

SWEET VALLEY KIDS™ DREAM BIRTHDAY GIFT SWEEPSTAKES

OFFICIAL ENTRY FORM

Name _____

Address _____

City _____ State _____ ZIP _____

Telephone No. _____

Date of Birth _____

CHOICE OF ONE DREAM BIRTHDAY GIFT:

BICYCLE _____ DOLLHOUSE _____ BALLET OUTFIT _____

OR

A GIFT OF YOUR CHOICE (maximum retail value: $500.00): _____

_____ .

Code: AN 80